Tea with Grandpa

BARNEY SALTZBERG

A NEAL PORTER BOOK
ROARING BROOK PRESS
NEW YORK

For Ella and her Baba Irv,
who gave his family the gifts of story, laughter, and love

Copyright © 2014 by Barney Saltzberg
A Neal Porter Book
Published by Roaring Brook Press
Roaring Brook Press is a division of Holtzbrinck Publishing Holdings Limited Partnership
175 Fifth Avenue, New York, New York 10010
mackids.com

Library of Congress Cataloging-in-Publication Data
Saltzberg, Barney, author, illustrator.
    Tea with Grandpa / Barney Saltzberg. — First edition.
        pages cm
    "A Neal Porter Book."
    Summary: No matter how far apart they are, a little girl and her
grandfather share a cup of tea every day at half past three.
    ISBN 978-1-59643-894-1 (hardcover)
[1. Stories in rhyme. 2. Grandfathers—Fiction. 3. Tea—Fiction. 4.
Internet—Fiction.] I. Title.
    PZ8.3.S174Te 2014
    [E]—dc23

                                                    2013001548

Roaring Brook Press books may be purchased for business or promotional use.
For information on bulk purchases please contact Macmillan Corporate and Premium Sales Department
at (800) 221-7945 x5442 or by email at specialmarkets@macmillan.com.

First edition 2014
Book design by Jennifer Browne
Printed in China by Macmillan Production (Asia) Ltd., Kowloon Bay, Hong Kong (supplier code 10)

1   3   5   7   9   10   8   6   4   2

Every day
at half past three . . .

Me and Grandpa. Time for tea.

I can pour
so carefully.

Grandpa holds
his cup for me.

He tells
me stories.

I sing a song.

Grandpa laughs
and sings along.

When I dance . . .

He laughs
some more.

I am a lion,

"I'd like some muffin," he will say.

I have to tell him,
"Too far away."

We clink our cups . . .

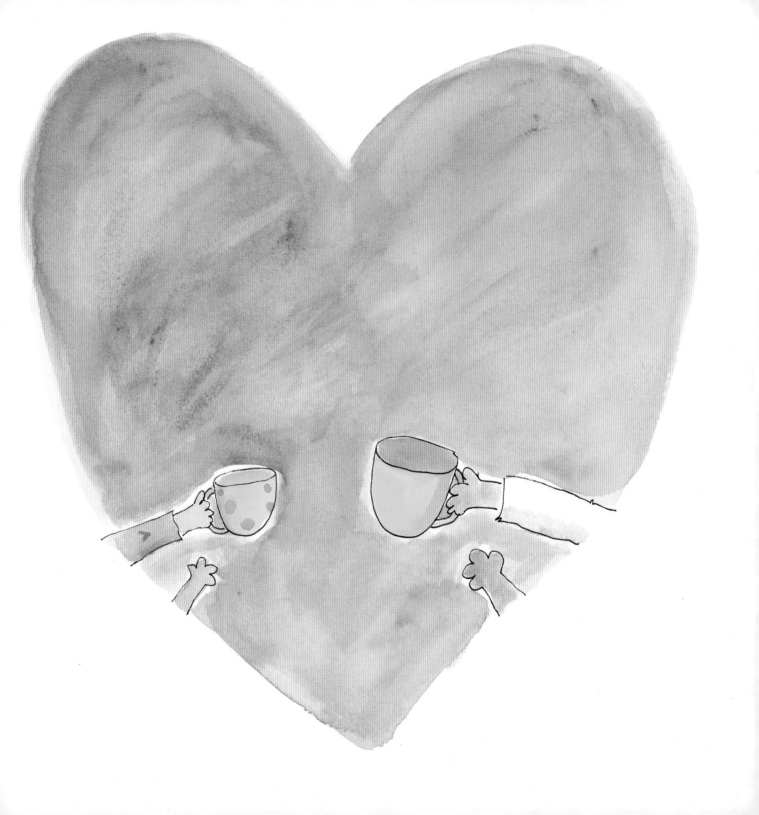

I say "Good-bye."

He says,
"Tomorrow,
sweetie pie."

'Cause every day
at half past
three . . .

Me and Grandpa,
time for tea.